Draw Me a Star

For my father (1904–1960)

Eric Carle Draw Me a Star

PUFFIN BOOKS

Draw me a star.

And the artist drew a star.

It was a good star.

Draw me the sun, said the star.
And the artist drew the sun.
It was a warm sun.

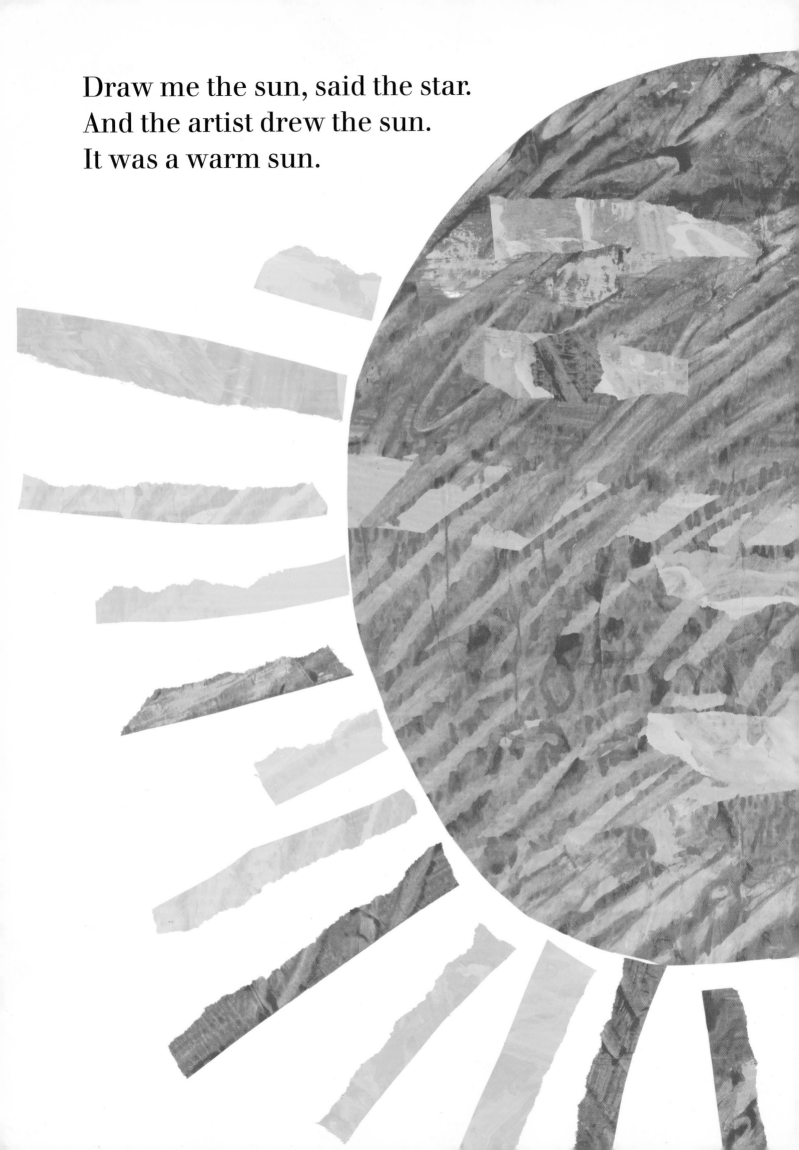

Draw me a tree, said the sun.
And the artist drew a tree.
It was a lovely tree.
Draw me a woman and a man.
And the artist drew a handsome couple.

Draw us a house, said the couple.
And the artist drew a house.
It was a strong house.

Draw me a dog, said the house.
And the artist drew a dog.
It was a big dog.

Draw me a cat, said the dog.
Draw me a bird, said the cat.
Draw me a butterfly, said the bird.

Draw me a flower, said the butterfly.
And the artist drew red and yellow
and blue and purple flowers.

Draw us a cloud, said the flowers.
And the artist drew clouds heavy with rain.

Draw me the night, said the rainbow.
And the artist drew a dark night.

Draw me the moon, said the night.
And the artist drew a full moon.
Draw me a star, said the moon.

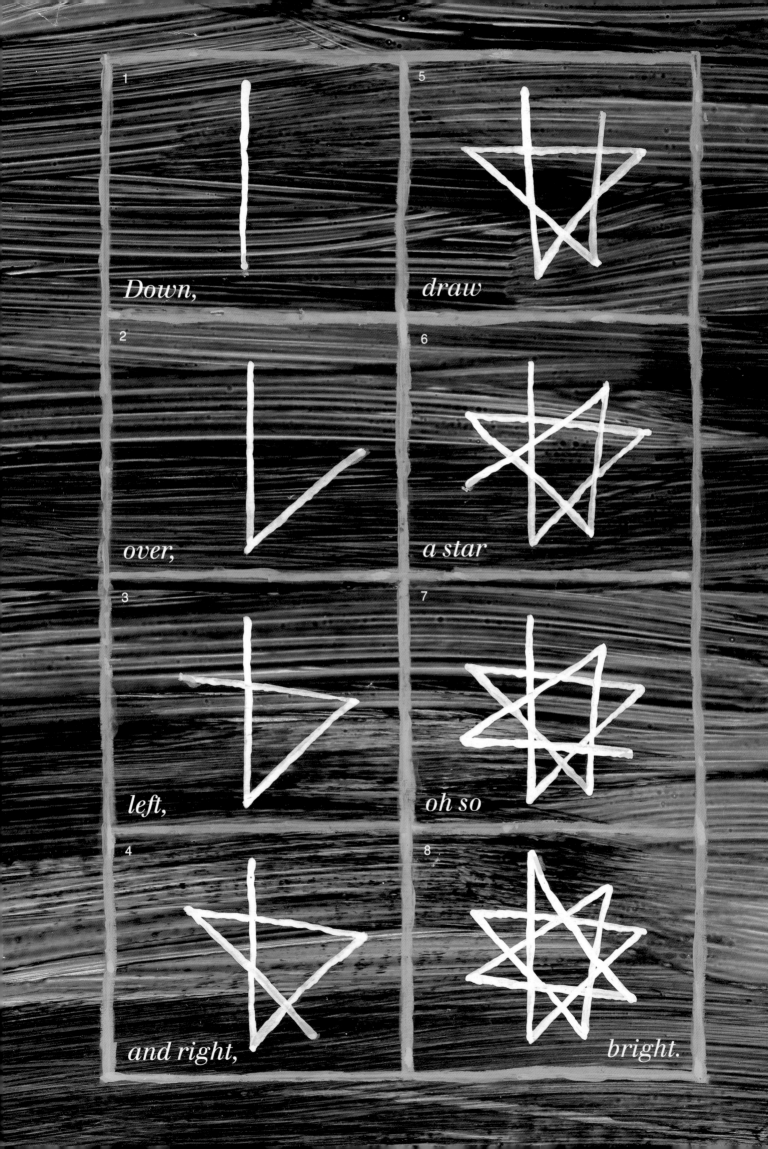

1 Down,

2 over,

3 left,

4 and right,

5 draw

6 a star

7 oh so

8 bright.

It was a good star.

Hold on to me, said the star to the artist.

Then, together, they traveled across the night sky.

Dear Friends,
When I was a young child my German Oma
(Grandmother) scribbled a star for me
as she recited this nonsense poem:

KRI KRA KROTEN- FUSS, GÄNSE LAUFEN BAR- FUSS
(KRI KRA TOAD'S FOOT, GEESE   WALK   BARE- FOOT)

Then last summer on my vacation,
I dreamed about shooting stars. The first
stars fell into the valleys of the distant
hills. More stars fell closer and closer.
Finally, a very bright star fell directly
on me, not hurting me at all; in fact,
it felt pleasant, kind of tingly. After
that the star and I rose up and
traveled across the night sky.
I had a beginning for a book, and an
ending. The middle was easy!

                    Sincerely,